Illustrated by Jerrod Maruyama

Customer Service: 1-877-277-9441 or customerservice@pikidsmedia.com

Published by PI Kids, an imprint of Phoenix International Publications, Inc.

8501 West Higgins Road   59 Gloucester Place   Heimhuder Straße 81
Chicago, Illinois 60631   London W1U 8JJ   20148 Hamburg

PI Kids is a trademark of Phoenix International Publications, Inc., and is registered in the United States.

www.pikidsmedia.com

ISBN: 978-1-5037-5814-8

Disney Growing UP Stories

June Gets a Job

A STORY ABOUT RESPONSIBILITY

An imprint of Phoenix International Publications, Inc.

Chicago • London • New York • Hamburg • Mexico City • Sydney

June loves to give her Aunt Daisy's dog, Jewel, a **BATH**.

"You're doing such a good job," says Minnie.
"The secret is having **TREATS** in your pocket,"
June says with a **GIGGLE**.

"How about a few customers?" asks Minnie. "Fifi could really use a bath."

"I'll wash her right now," says June.

"That goes for Pluto, too!" Mickey says.

"Hmm," says Daisy. "This sounds like the start of a little business."

June thinks this is a **GREAT** idea.

"What do you think, Pluto?" June asks.
Pluto answers with a loud WOOF!

Soon, word of mouth reaches their neighbors and friends. Everyone wants an appointment for their pooch. June's new job *TAKES OFF!*

The next day, Jewel has an appointment for a **BATH**. As June gets the pup ready, her sisters April and May join them in the yard.

ARF!

"Don't forget we're having a picnic at NOON today,"
says May.
"I'll be ready," replies June.

Just as June puts Jewel in the tub, a squirrel runs through the yard. **Jewel wants to play!** She *CHASES* after the squirrel, *RUNS* through the open fence, and *RACES* down the sidewalk.

SQUEAK!

ARF!

Jewel stops to sniff the ground, but as soon as June gets close, she **RUNS OFF AGAIN!**

June returns home just before noon, **without Jewel**.

"We have to leave right now!" says April. "Our friends are waiting for us."

June doesn't want to make her sisters late. But she doesn't know what to do about Jewel!

When June explains what happened, Daisy has an idea.

"I'll ask Donald, Mickey, and Minnie to help me look around the neighborhood for Jewel," she says. "You three go have your picnic."

SIGH!

At the park, the girls set out their picnic lunch. Soon, everyone is busy **LAUGHING** and **EATING**—**except June**.

"You're awfully quiet, June," says May.

June feels bad that she isn't helping Aunt Daisy. "I'm going to look for Jewel at the pond," she says. **"That's her favorite spot!"**

As June gets near the pond, she sees Clarabelle with her three dogs, Cissy, Chrissy, and Missy. **And she sees Jewel!**

The dogs **RUN** in circles, trying to chase the geese. Clarabelle gets **TANGLED** up in the leashes.

"Oh, dear," she says. "Can somebody please unwind me?"

June **HURRIES** over to help Clarabelle.
She pulls some biscuits out of her pocket and
tells the dogs to sit as she **UNTANGLES**
the leashes.

"Thank goodness for **TREATS**!" says June,
as she scoops up Jewel and gives her a hug.

Just then, Daisy and her friends arrive.

"You found Jewel!" says Daisy.

Jewel is panting and happy. She's **ROLLED** in so much **MUD** on her adventure, she's really dirty now!

"Looks like Jewel needs another bath," says Daisy.

"She's going to be *my first and last* customer of the day," says June.

"I'd like to hire you too," says Clarabelle. "I can see that you're **GREAT** with dogs."

"I'd be happy to wash Chrissy, Cissy, and Missy," says June. "But first, I need to get Jewel into the tub... *RIGHT AWAY!*"

Back home, June gives Jewel the **BEST BATH EVER.**

POP! POP!

"I'm really proud of you for taking your job so seriously," says Daisy.

"Being responsible is important to me," says June. "And I want everyone to know it!"

"ARF! ARF!" Jewel agrees.